Be Brave, Little Penguin

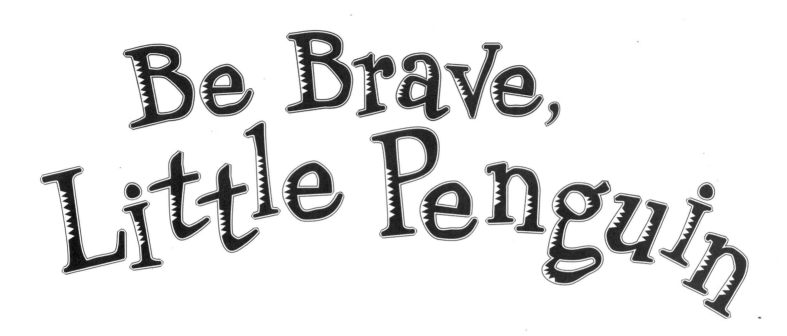

Library of Congress Cataloging-in-Publication Data available

ISBN 978-1-338-15039-1

10 9 8 7 6 5 4 3 2 1   18 19 20 21 22

Printed in China   38
This edition first printing, January 2018

For our own little penguins. May you always
find the courage to jump! – G.A.

For my brave boys: Joe, James, and Dylan – G.P.R.

Be Brave, Little Penguin

GILES ANDREAE   GUY PARKER-REES

ORCHARD BOOKS
An Imprint of Scholastic Inc.
New York

In the cold Antarctic sunshine,
Where the icy ocean ends,
Lived a family of penguins,
With all their penguin friends.

There were FAT ones.
There were THIN ones.
There were penguins
SHoRT and TALL,

But little penguin Pip-Pip
Was the SMALLEST one of all.

And while the other penguins
Were out swimming wild and free,
Little Pip-Pip played alone,
Too frightened of the sea.

Names like "SCAREDY-PIP-PIP"
Echoed in his ears.
He was SAD and he was LONELY,
But he couldn't show his tears.

"What's the matter, Pip-Pip?"
Said his daddy one fine day.

"You can't be scared of water!
What a silly thing to say!"

"Be gentle," said his mommy,
Taking Pip-Pip by the hand.
"We ALL have certain fears
That might be hard to understand.

Come on, little Pip-Pip,
Dip your toes in here, just so.
The water's calm and still now.
You can do it. Nice and slow."

"But what if the water's FREEZING?

Mommy, what if I get in

And it's just too dark and deep for me?

And what if . . . I CAN'T swim?

What if in that water

There are friends for you to meet?

And what if it is LIGHT and WARM

And full of treats to eat?"

"Take my hand, my little one.
Don't worry — I'm right here.
Please trust me, little Pip-Pip.
Be BRAVE — and never fear."

Slowly, Pip-Pip made his way
Toward the water's edge.
He stared down at the ocean
From the slippery, icy ledge.

Then he looked back
at his mommy,
And as his small
heart thumped,
He closed his eyes,
he held his breath,
And little Pip-Pip . . .

... JUMPED!

For a while, his mommy waited.

Then she cried out, "Something's wrong!

Pip-Pip, please, where are you? You've been under way too long!"

So she leaped into the ocean,
Diving deep into the blue.

Then suddenly, from nowhere,
Came a little voice she knew.

"Mommy, Mommy, over here!
Hey, Mommy, look at me!
I'm swimming, Mommy, swimming!
Look, I'm SWIMMING!
Can you see?"

She TURNED and, SPINNING CIRCLES
Through the water bright and clean,

Swam Pip-Pip, with the BIGGEST smile
The world has ever seen!

And as she watched her little one,
Right there before her eyes,
He burst up through the surface

And he SOARED into the skies!

"Oh, Pip-Pip," laughed his mommy,
As she watched him with a grin.
"I don't know about flying,
But, oh my . . . you've learned to SWIM!"

Then his friends all gathered 'round
As Pip-Pip landed with a BUMP,

And said,
"Sometimes all you have to do
Is just be BRAVE . . .